Pippa Pennington
Sniffer at the Farm

Illustrated by Eitatsu

Sniffer loved to sniff, and the things he loved most of all were the smelliest things he could find. His nose would go up in the air at the slightest whiff and he'd sniff.

He couldn't help going in search to find out what was causing such a smelly smell.

"Sniffer, that nose of yours will get you in trouble one day," his mum told him.

Sniffer didn't listen. His mum didn't know about sniffing. He wanted to sniff all day long. His best times were when he was sniffing.

What trouble could it cause?

Sniffer's nose always went up in the air.

Sniff, sniff, sniff. Phew! What is that?

One morning he looked around the garden. Now would be a good time to go and do some serious sniffing.

He checked around the garden again before digging a hole under the fence. He always got into lots of trouble for digging, but the smell was so good, he couldn't help himself. Naughty Sniffer!

Sniffer trotted along the path, stopping when he smelled something good.

He lifted his head up. Sniff, sniff, sniff. Phew! What is that?

Sniffer saw a gate. It was open just a little bit. Should he go in?

The smell was lovely. Sniff, sniff, sniff.
Phew! What is that? He had to go in and find out.

Sniffer kept his nose to the ground as he trotted across the field. The smell was getting stronger. Moo! Moo! A big cow looked at Sniffer. She didn't look happy.

Whoa! The cow was big and Sniffer was frightened. He ran away as fast as he could. His nose went up in the air. Sniff, sniff, sniff. What is that?

Sniffer saw a big, brown pile of cow whoopsy. Sniff, sniff, sniff. Cor! It smelled so good.

Sniffer looked around to make sure the cow wasn't near. He bent down and rubbed the whoopsy all over himself. Phew! It smelled so good. Naughty Sniffer!

Sniffer ran on across the field. He was having such fun today. His nose went up in the air. Sniff, sniff, sniff. Phew! What is that?

Sniffer saw a fence and a shed. Phew! That must be the smelliest smell ever!

Sniffer trotted over to the shed. He looked at the fence. He had to find that smell. Should he go under the fence?

Sniffer crawled under the fence and put his nose to the ground. It was so smelly. Lovely!

Sniffer didn't look where he was going. He sniffed and sniffed. Suddenly, his nose touched something. Sniffer lifted his head and a big, black pig looked at him.

"Oink! Oink! Oink!" said the pig.

"Oink! Oink! Oink!" The pig didn't look happy.
The pig pushed its nose under Sniffer's tummy.
Oh no! What's happening?

The pig tossed Sniffer up in the air.

Sniffer crawled back under the fence and shook off all the mud and straw. The pig didn't have to do that. How rude!

Now Sniffer's bottom hurt. He wouldn't go and visit the pig again.

Sniffer ran across the farmyard. Sniff, sniff, sniff. Phew! What is that?

Sniffer followed the smell and saw a field of sheep.

Baa! Baa! Baa! The sheep looked nice and gentle. Nothing to hurt him in this field. Sniffer went under the fence. The horse watched.

Sniffer ran across the field with his nose to the ground. Sniff, sniff, sniff. Something smelled good.

Oh no! Sniffer isn't looking where he's going.
Who can you see?

Suddenly Sniffer was flying through the air. Whoa! Oh no! Not again.

Sniffer landed on his bottom. "Ouch!' He looked up and saw a goat with two big horns. Oh no! The goat walked towards Sniffer. Run Sniffer! Run!

Sniffer looked this way and that way. Which way would be safe? The farm was a dangerous place. All he wanted to do was sniff.

Sniffer stopped running. Sniff, sniff, sniff.
What is that?

Suddenly Sniffer heard a noise. Gobble, gobble, gobble. Whoa! What was that?

Sniffer was too frightened to look around. Gobble, gobble, gobble. Sniffer ran. Who can you see?

A big turkey chased Sniffer. Sniffer ran as fast as he could.

The turkey was getting closer. Run Sniffer!

Run!

The horse watched.

Sniffer ran back past the goat.

Back past the pig.

Back past the cow.

The turkey still chased him.

Sniffer wished he was safe at home in his garden.

Sniffer ran all the way home. "Sniffer, where have you been?" Mum said.

"Sorry. I didn't listen to you," he said. "I was flying, and then a monster chased me."

"Really? I think you need to think about listening. It's dangerous to go sniffing," Mum said.

"I don't ever want to go sniffing again," Sniffer said.

Sniffer went to his kennel. He fell asleep and dreamed of cows, goats and turkeys. Was that the pig he could smell? Or was it the whoopsy the cow did? It was so lovely and smelly rolling in that smelly mess.

Sniffer's nose started to twitch.

Suddenly Sniffer opened one eye and his nose went up in the air. Sniff, sniff, sniff. What is that?

Oh no! What do you think Sniffer will do next?

More picture books by Pippa Pennington:

Sniffer

Sniffer's nose leads him into trouble when he goes for a walk. A smelly sock and a rubbish bin have lovely smells, but when Growler, the big dog from next door, wants the blue cheese, Sniffer has to run.

Sniffer at the Beach

Sniffer's nose leads him to the beach where he finds himself in trouble with crabs, sandcastles, fishermen and seaweed. Then... Worst of all... The dog catcher. Run, Sniffer! Run!

Sniffer's First Christmas

Sniffer finds himself in trouble when he helps himself to the mince pies and turkey. He couldn't help himself... They smelled so good.

Join my mailing list for free e-books, news of new releases, and special offers.
http://book.adventureswithsniffer.com/